anythink

anythink

Boris and Stella
and the Perfect Gift

By Dara Goldman

Text Copyright and Illustration Copyright © 2013 Dara Goldman
Illustrations were created using pencil and watercolor.

Sleeping Bear Press™
315 E. Eisenhower Parkway, Suite 200
Ann Arbor, MI 48108
www.sleepingbearpress.com

Printed and bound in the United States.

10 9 8 7 6 5 4 3 2 1

Library of Congress Cataloging-in-Publication Data

Goldman, Dara, author, illustrator.
Boris and Stella and the perfect gift / written and illustrated by Dara Goldman.
pages cm
Summary: Boris and Stella are in love but do not have much money, so Stella sells
something very important to her in order to buy Boris a Hanukkah gift, and Boris does
likewise to buy Stella a Christmas present.
ISBN 978-1-58536-859-4
[1. Gifts—Fiction. 2. Hanukkah—Fiction. 3. Christmas—Fiction.] I. Henry, O., 1862-1910.
Gift of the Magi. II. Title. III. Title: Perfect gift.
PZ7.G5679Bor 2013
[E]—dc23
2013002578

To Libby

Boris and Stella lived in the city. Boris played the piano every night in the little restaurant downstairs. He played music that he learned when he was growing up in Russia.

Stella adored his music.

Stella was a baker. She baked cakes in the little shop next door.

Boris adored cake.

They both liked hats ...

...and scary movies.
It was true love.

Hanukkah was almost here and Stella wanted to give Boris something special. She shook her savings bank upside down. Only a few coins fell out. How could she give Boris something special if she only had a few coins?

She looked around the little apartment. All she had of value was a pine tree from her family's farm in Italy. Her papa had given it to her when it was a seedling. It reminded Stella of her home and family during Christmas.

Suddenly, Stella had an idea.

She put on her favorite hat, picked up her tree, and carried it down a long flight of stairs.

The owner of the flower shop next door was happy to buy Stella's tree. It was just the right size for his shop window. Stella didn't need a tree to remind her of her family during Christmas. They were always in her heart. The shopkeeper paid Stella enough money so she could buy Boris a special gift.

Stella knew exactly what she wanted to give Boris for Hanukkah. She hurried across town to a shop that sold dreidels. The shopkeeper had only one left. It was from Israel. The Hebrew letters on dreidels sold in Israel stood for "A Great Miracle Happened Here." Stella thought it was a miracle that she had met Boris. It was the perfect gift!

Boris was troubled too. It was almost Christmas and he still didn't have a gift for Stella. Boris wanted to give her something special for Christmas.

He shook his savings bank upside down. Only a few coins fell out. How could he give Stella something special if he only had a few coins?

Boris looked around the tiny apartment. The only thing he had of value was his dreidel collection. His mama and papa gave him one every Hanukkah when he was growing up in Russia. They reminded him of his home and family.

All of a sudden, Boris had an idea.

He put on his favorite hat, and took his dreidel collection across town. The owner of the gift shop there was happy to buy his dreidels. He had just sold his last one to a customer a few minutes earlier and he didn't have any left.

Boris got enough money to buy Stella a special gift. He didn't need the dreidels to remind him of his family during Hanukkah. They would always be in his heart.

Boris knew exactly what he wanted to give Stella. The little flower shop next door had a beautiful Christmas tree in the window. On the top was a dazzling glass star. It would be beautiful on top of Stella's tree!

Stella was a dazzling star to Boris. And Stella meant star in Italian. It was the perfect gift.

This year, the eighth night of Hanukkah fell on Christmas eve. Boris made delicious potato latkes the way his mama made them in Russia. He served them with a giant dollop of sour cream on top, just the way Stella liked them.

Stella made a panettone cake like the ones her papa used to make in Italy. She filled it with hazelnuts and topped it with chocolate, just the way Boris liked it.

The last night of Hanukkah was Stella's favorite because she and Boris could light all the candles in his menorah. The room glowed orange. Big, fluffy snowflakes fell outside. It was a perfect Hanukkah-Christmas night, but... something was missing. Then Boris noticed what it was.

"Where is your tree?" he asked Stella.

Stella gave a small box to Boris.

"I sold it to buy this for you," she said happily.

Inside the box Boris found a beautiful dreidel.
He threw his arms in the air, "Bozhe moi!"
he said in Russian. Oh no!

Stella looked over at the fireplace mantel.

"Where are your dreidels?" she asked Boris.

Boris presented a box to Stella.

"I sold them to buy this for you," he said.

Inside the box Stella found a brilliant glass star for the top of the Christmas tree she didn't have anymore!

"Mamma mia!" she said in Italian.

Boris put his new dreidel on the mantel.

"This is the beginning of our new dreidel collection," he said. "It's going to be magnificent."

Boris always knew exactly what to say to make Stella feel better.

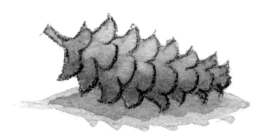

Then she noticed something lying in the corner. It was a small pinecone that had dropped from her tree. Inside there were seeds.

"Look, Boris!" Stella said. "We will grow a new Christmas tree!"

Stella always knew just what to say to make Boris feel better.